What If?

What

by **Else Holmelund Minarik**
pictures by
Margaret Bloy Graham

If?

Greenwillow Books, New York

Library of Congress Cataloging-in-Publication Data
Minarik, Else Holmelund.   What if?
Summary: Tossed out of the house, two cats
fantasize about what would happen if they
had their own Christmas tree.
[1. Cats—Fiction.
2. Christmas trees—Fiction]
I. Graham, Margaret Bloy, ill.   II. Title.
PZ8.M652Wh   1987   [E]   86-7649
ISBN 0-688-06473-6
ISBN 0-688-06474-4 (lib. bdg.)

Watercolor and gouache paints and colored
pencils were used for the full-color art.
The text type is Weideman Medium.

For Zuleika,
Homer,
and Susan

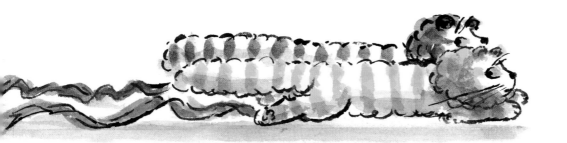

Pit and Pat
were tossed
out of the house.

They scuffled around a bit in the snow.

Then Pit said to Pat,
"What if we had a tree of our own?"

"Our own Christmas tree!" said Pat.
"And what if it reached the sky?" said Pit.

"And what if we picked a star
for its top?" said Pat.

"And what if we trimmed it," said Pit,

"with ice mice and icicles!" said Pat.

"And what if we found a silver slide
   at the top?" said Pit.
"And slid down the slide," said Pat,

"round and round and down and down,"
said Pit,
"through all the branches!" said Pat.

"And landed in a nest," said Pit,

"of little kitten birds," said Pat.

"And grew wings of our own," said Pit,

"and flew about," said Pat.

"And lost our wings," said Pit,
"and lost our tree," said Pat.

"And fell in the snow," said Pit,
"right where we are now," finished Pat.

Pat and Pit looked at each other.
Pit said, "What if we scratch on the door,"
"and they let us in!" said Pat.

Pit and Pat scratched on the door —

AND THE DOOR OPENED.